THE RAGGY DOLLS

THE ROYAL TOUR

FROM AN ORIGINAL IDEA BY
MELVYN JACOBSON

ADAPTED BY
NEIL INNES

ILLUSTRATED BY
STEVE SMALLMAN

YORKSHIRE
TELEVISION

BOXTREE LTD

THE RAGGY DOLLS

The Raggy Dolls live in the Reject Bin
in Mr Grimes's toy factory . . .

HI-FI was a talking doll, but when he was being tested, someone dropped him. He can still talk – but only with a stammer.

First published in Great Britain in 1990
By Boxtree Limited
Published in association with Yorkshire Television Limited

Text © Yorkshire Television 1990
Illustrations © Boxtree Limited 1990

The RAGGY DOLLS is a Trademark of Yorkshire Television Limited
© Melvyn Jacobson Productions Ltd

British Library Cataloguing in Publication Data
Innes, Neil
 The Royal tour.
 I. Title II. Smallman, Steve   III. Series
823'.914 [F]

ISBN 1-85283-045-X

Designed by Bet Ayer
Edited by Cheryl Brown
Typeset by Tradespools Limited, Frome, Somerset
Origination by Culvergraphics

For Boxtree Limited
36 Tavistock Street, London WC2E 7PB

BACK-TO-FRONT was a handy man doll with a complete tool-kit, but somehow the machine put his head on the wrong way round.

LUCY was sewn together with faulty thread. Now her joints are so loose, she goes to pieces if she gets excited.

DOTTY was perfect in every way – until she got splashed with paint that would not come off.

CLAUDE is a French doll. There is nothing wrong with him. He was part of a special export order to France, but the machine made one too many – and he was left behind.

PRINCESS should have had a tiara, beautiful hair, and a splendid dress – but the machine went wrong, dressed her in rags and cropped her hair.

SAD SACK was a sample, but because he was nice and plump, he used up too much stuffing. This made him expensive, so nobody wanted him.

One morning, Princess looked in the mirror. "Ho dear," she sighed. "Hi don't know why hi'm called Princess. Hi don't look royal hat hall. Hi look just like heverybody helse."

"You should wear brighter clothes," said Dotty.

"And do a lot of smiling," suggested Lucy.

So Princess practised smiling – it made her jaw ache.

"Try shaking hands with us all," said Back-to-Front.

So Princess shook hands with all the Raggy Dolls until her arm ached – but she still didn't look royal.

"Would a crown help?" asked Lucy.

"Crowns are for Queens," said Dotty, "but Princess could wear a coronet."

"I 'ave an idea," said Claude. "Leave eet to me, mes amis."

"And me," whispered Lucy.

Claude went into the canteen kitchen and found some flour and a bowl. He soon mixed up some dough and began shaping it.

Meanwhile, Lucy had gone to the store room and found some oddments of material. There was quite a lot of shiny red silk. "Oh, this is really royal," she thought. She took some scissors and began cutting out a pattern.

By lunchtime, Princess had a beautiful red silk dress. And a coronet baked out of bread, decorated with ruby cherries and diamond sugar crystals.

Princess was delighted. "Let's do something hexciting!" she exclaimed. "Something habsolutely royal."

"What about g-g-going on a t-t-tour?" suggested Hi-Fi.

"Good thinking," said Dotty.

The Raggy Dolls decided that Princess ought to have a carriage. At first they thought a doll's pram would be ideal, but Princess didn't want to go in a carriage all by herself. If she was going on a Royal Tour, she wanted all her Raggy Doll friends to come with her.

"We can take ha picnic," she said.

"Where are we going to find a carriage big enough to take all seven of us *and* a picnic?" demanded Sad Sack.

"No problem," said Back-to-Front." We'll make one – there are lots of wheels and useful things in the tool shed."

"Good thinking," said Dotty. "Come on everyone, let's get cracking!"

The Raggy Dolls happily set to work building a carriage fit for a Princess, a picnic and six friends.

When it was finished, it looked more like a long bicycle than a carriage. The Raggy Dolls climbed on and waited for Princess to take her seat of honour.

The Raggy Dolls all saluted as Princess climbed aboard and after a somewhat wobbly start, the Royal Tour was begun.

The first person they met was Pumpernickel, the scarecrow.

"My word, you do look grand!" he said when he saw Princess.

"We're hon ha Royal Tour," she proudly announced.

"Well, thanks for visiting me," said Pumpernickel with a bow. "It's an honour, that's what it is. Who are you going to see next?"

The Raggy Dolls looked at each other and blinked. They had forgotten to plan where they were going.

"Um, we haven't decided yet," said Dotty.

"Then why don't you visit my cousin Tabitha?" said Pumpernickel. "She'll be tickled pink!"

And to make sure the Raggy Dolls didn't lose their way, he gave them a map. Every scarecrow on Farmer Brown's land was marked with a cross, including Cousin Tabitha.

Pedalling the carriage was quite hard work. The Raggy Dolls soon had to stop for a rest.

"That's the trouble with maps," thought Sad Sack puffing heavily, "they always show places nearer to places than they really are."

He was about to tell the others what he thought of maps when Dotty decided it was time to go.

Thanks to Pumpernickel's map, the Raggy Dolls soon found Cousin Tabitha. She was standing in the middle of a field looking very cross. The wind had blown her hat away, and her dress was hanging in shreds.

"Those darn crows," she screeched. "They does it on purpose, that they do. They've no respect. They pecks and pecks and pulls bits off me and lines their nests with me petticoats. Oh, how they do aggravate me!"

Sad Sack thought Cousin Tabitha looked more like a witch than a scarecrow.

"Er . . . we're on a Royal Tour," explained Lucy.

"P-P-Pumpernickel sends you g-g-greetings," said Hi-Fi.

"Oh he does, does he? Well you tell 'im to send more petticoats," grumbled Cousin Tabitha. "They're a darn sight more use than greetings." The Raggy Dolls thought she was a very disagreeable creature.

Dotty studied Pumpernickel's map. "Let's visit some of the other scarecrows," she whispered, "perhaps they will be more pleasant." Everyone agreed, and even Sad Sack was glad to be on his way again.

Soon they reached the spot where the next scarecrow should be.

BANG! The Raggy Dolls jumped in fright. Instead of finding a pleasant scarecrow to talk to, they found an automatic bird-scarer.

"Let's be on our way," said Dotty, "before it goes off again!"

The next scarecrow was disappointing too. The Raggy Dolls couldn't talk to it because it had no face. It was made of two broom handles hung with metal strips that tinkled in the breeze.

"What about having our picnic here?" suggested Sad Sack.

"Good thinking," said Dotty. Everyone helped to unpack the hamper. There were sausages and jam tarts and bottles of lemonade.

No one noticed the magpie until it was too late. It swooped down, grabbed Princess's coronet in its greedy claws and flew up into a tree.

First it ate the ruby cherries, then the sugar diamonds, then it scoffed the circle of bread. Not a crumb was left.

"Ho no!" wailed Princess.

Princess wandered off on her own, trying very hard not to cry. Suddenly she heard a strange huffing and puffing. "Ho dear," she gasped. Standing very near her, looking very fierce, was a very large brown bull!

"HELP!" she cried.

"Raggy Dolls to the rescue!" shouted Dotty.

The Raggy Dolls leapt on to the carriage and pedalled for all they were worth, scooping up Princess on the way. They travelled so fast that when they hit a big bump, the carriage took off and flew over the hedge, leaving the bull stamping and snorting on the other side.

Sadly, the carriage wasn't meant to fly and when it landed, it was beyond repair. The Royal Tour was over.

"It must have been your red dress," panted Back-to-Front.

"Yes," agreed Dotty, catching her breath, "bulls go mad when they see red."

Everyone felt sorry for Princess. Her big day had been ruined. "Never mind," she said bravely. "Hi've had henough hexcitement to last ha lifetime. Hi want to go home hand be hordinary hagain."

It was a long walk home carrying the broken carriage, and when they got there the Raggy Dolls put all the bits back in the tool shed.

Back in the reject bin, Princess put on her old dress and handed the shiny red one to Lucy. "Hi'm sorry Lucy," she said, "hit's han hadorable dress but hi can't wear hit hanymore."

"Don't worry," said Lucy, with a grin, "I think I know someone who can!"